ONE
WORLD
TOGETHER

F
FRANCES LINCOLN
CHILDREN'S BOOKS

I want a friend. Who will I choose?

I went to Brazil.

I met a boy called Paulo.

Where does Paulo live? High in the sky.

Paulo's dad has a cool motorbike.

Everyone in Brazil loves football.

And especially Paulo!

Paulo would be a GOOD friend.

Mohamed plays in the street with his friends.

Mohamed helps his father in the market,

and he gives a carrot to their donkey.

Mohamed would be a GOOD friend too.

Lukas walks to school with his friends.

"There are lots of wonderful animals in Kenya," he says.

"We must not waste water," says Lukas.

Lukas sleeps under a mosquito net. Goodnight, Lukas.

Lukas would be a GOOD friend too.

Sophie and Sem like anything with two wheels.

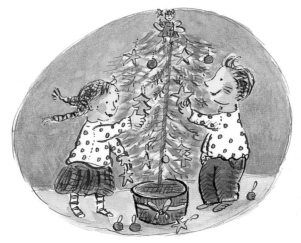

Their favourite time
is Christmas.

Their mother is a doctor.
Sophie wants to be a doctor too.

The twins love to ride on the
canal boat.

Look! Sophie and Sem have
a secret house in the garden.

Sophie and Sem would be GOOD friends too.

 I went to Sweden.

I met a girl called Lilly.

Lilly lives in a red wooden house.

She is learning to play the recorder.

Her favourite book is 'Pippi Longstocking',

and her favourite person is her new baby sister.

Lilly would be a GOOD friend too.

Galina has a doll inside a doll inside a doll.

Galina wakes up early
and makes a lot of noise.

"See this?" she says.
"I've won a Special Prize
For Dancing."

Her mum is going to have a baby.

Galina would be a GOOD friend too.

 I went to India.

I met a girl called Vani.

Vani wants to be a famous singer,

in a beautiful sari
with lots of bracelets.

Vani's mother puts oil
in her hair to make it
beautiful and shiny.

"The rainy season is called the monsoon," says Vani.

Vani would be a GOOD friend too.

Li loves to watch the Dragon Dance.

"There are more people in China than any country in the world," says Li.

Li likes computer games.

She plays ping-pong with her dad.

She eats her food with chopsticks.

Li would be a GOOD friend too.

Yuuki and his friends bow to their teacher.

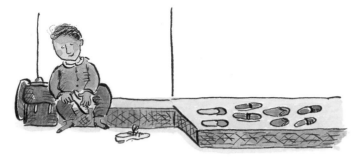

He takes his shoes off when he goes inside his house.

He loves to eat sushi.

"My favourite day is Children's Day," says Yuuki.

Yuuki would make a GOOD friend too.

I want a friend.

But who will I choose?